W9-AUQ-953

CAPTAIN CAT

CAPTAIN CAT

Story and pictures by
SYD HOFF

HarperTrophy®
A Division of HarperCollins*Publishers*

Captain Cat
Copyright © 1993 by Syd Hoff
Printed in the United States of America. All rights reserved.
For information address HarperCollins
Children's Books, a division of HarperCollins Publishers,
10 East 53rd Street, New York, NY 10022.
❖
Library of Congress Cataloging-in-Publication Data
Hoff, Syd, date
    Captain Cat : story and pictures / by Syd Hoff.
        p.   cm. —(An I can read book)
    Summary: A cat makes friends with a soldier and learns about military life
when he joins the army.
    ISBN 0-06-020527-X. — ISBN 0-06-020528-8 (lib. bdg.)
    ISBN 0-06-444176-8 (pbk.)
    [1. Cats—Fiction.   2. United States. Army—Fiction.]   I. Title.
II. Series.
PZ7.H672Cap   1993   91-27518
[E]—dc20   CIP
                                                                        AC

13 LP/WOR 20 19 18 17 16

For Nina

Captain Cat joined the army.

He went in when nobody was looking.

The soldiers marched in a parade.

"Left, right—

left, right . . ."

Captain Cat kept in step.

He knew one foot from the other.

"That cat has more stripes

than we have,"

said a corporal to a sergeant.

12

"Meow," said Captain Cat.

Another sergeant looked at the cat.

"Yes sir!" he said and laughed.

From then on
everybody started saying,
"Here, Captain Cat,"
when they wanted him,
instead of
"Here, kitty kitty."

But sometimes the soldiers

had no time for Captain Cat.

16

"I have to clean the bathrooms,"

said one soldier.

"I have to sweep the grounds,"

said another soldier.

ne soldier named Pete

lways found time for Captain Cat,

ven when he was on guard duty.

You remind me of a cat back home,"

e said, and scratched Captain Cat

ehind the ears.

19

Pete played with Captain Cat so mu

he got into trouble.

The general made Pete

do kitchen duty.

Captain Cat kept him company.

Pete let Captain Cat play

with the potato peels.

"Are you my buddy?"

asked Pete.

"Me-ow," said Captain Cat.

The next morning

a bugle blew.

Oh, how Pete hated to get up!

24

But Captain Cat

sprang right out of bed.

25

He had to check out the garbage

before it was taken away.

Then it was time for inspection.

Everybody lined up.

28

Captain Cat lined up, too.

The general fixed a soldier's gun.

30

He fixed Pete's hat.

All he could fix for Captain Cat were his whiskers.

"Forward march!" said the general.

The soldiers went one way.

Captain Cat went the other way.

He had to chase some birds.

The soldiers crawled

in the mud.

They hiked

through rain and sleet.

But not Captain Cat!
He was taking a nap
on Pete's bed.

39

Time for chow!

Pete and the other soldiers

rushed into the mess hall

to get plates of nice, hot food.

Captain Cat wished

Pete would get him

a plate with a mouse.

"Are you my buddy?" asked Pete.

"Me-ow," said Captain Cat.

Lights out!

Everyone went to sleep

and dreamed of loved ones.

44

45

Captain Cat dreamed

of his loved one, too.

46